For Sami —B. H.

To Alon, a shark expert —G. B.

Henry Holt and Company, *Publishers since 1866*

Henry Holt® is a registered trademark of Macmillan Publishing Group, LLC.

120 Broadway, New York, NY 10271 · mackids.com

Text copyright © 2021 by Bridget Heos

Illustrations copyright © 2021 by Galia Bernstein

All rights reserved

Library of Congress Cataloging-in-Publication Data is available.

Our books may be purchased in bulk for promotional, educational, or business use.

Please contact your local bookseller or the Macmillan Corporate and Premium Sales Department

at (800) 221-7945 ext. 5442 or by email at MacmillanSpecialMarkets@macmillan.com.

First Edition, 2021

Printed in China by RR Donnelley Asia Printing Solutions Ltd., Dongguan City, Guangdong Province.

ISBN 978-1-250-24462-8

1 3 5 7 9 10 8 6 4 2

SANTA JAWS

Written by **Bridget Heos**

Illustrated by **Galia Bernstein**

HENRY HOLT AND COMPANY
New York

While kids write notes to Santa Claus,
Sharks line up for Santa Jaws.

They tell him all their Christmas wishes.
Santa thinks they sound delicious!

Pups awaiting, elfin sharks
Toil in workshops deep and dark,
Making toys from shelly things—
A seal that squeaks, a ray that stings.

Meanwhile, in the golden sands,
Sharks make winter wonderlands.

Horn sharks trim the Christmas kelp
And top it (with a little help).

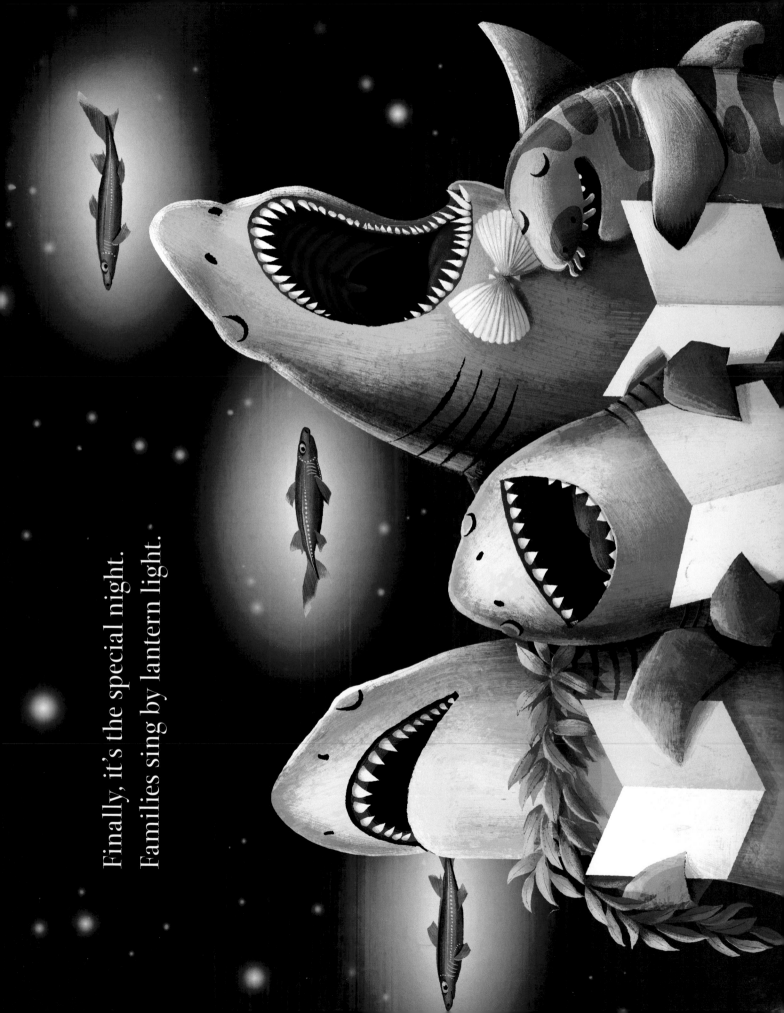

Finally, it's the special night.
Families sing by lantern light.

Cookiecutter sharks make treats

For Santa and his Christmas fleet.

Tiny carpet sharks are wrestled
Into seabeds where, once nestled,
They dream of Christmas delicacies
Drifting 'cross the darkening seas.

Then Santa boards his merry sled
Pulled by hungry hammerheads,

Up to reeftops, swish, swish, swish, swish,
Down to seabeds for fish, fish, fish.

He takes in all the festive sights—
Chewy wreaths, crunchy lights.

At last, he opens up his net.
What will little reef sharks get?

He checks the list. Naughty? Nice?
Yum! He'd better check it twice!

For good sharks,
He brings toys delish,

For bad pups,
Weeds and rotten fish.

He stuffs each sharkling's stocking tight
And tests the toys—just a bite.

Upon the yuletide, he swims away,
With leagues to go by break of day.

Pups awaking to a jingle
Search the tide for old Shark Kringle.

Waving a fin, he roars a good night:
**FISHY CHRISTMAS TO ALL,
AND TO ALL A GOOD BITE!**

There are over five hundred species of known sharks, with more being discovered all the time. **Eight appear in this story.**

ELFIN SHARKS, also known as goblin sharks, are named for their pointy, turned-up noses. They live in the deep sea.

HORN SHARKS live near the seabed in kelp forests.

LANTERN SHARKS (the small sharks lighting the way for the singing sharks) are bioluminescent.

COOKIECUTTER SHARKS suck on their prey, leaving behind round circles of missing flesh.

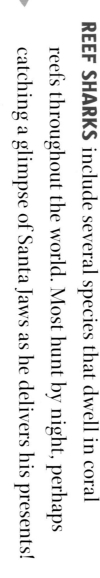

CARPET SHARKS are not a species, but rather a group of many types of sharks that usually hide in the seabed, stealthily awaiting their prey.

HAMMERHEADS often swim in schools by day. Unlike in this story, they keep to themselves at night.

REEF SHARKS include several species that dwell in coral reefs throughout the world. Most hunt by night, perhaps catching a glimpse of Santa Jaws as he delivers his presents!

GREAT WHITE SHARKS, like Santa Jaws, are known for taste testing a variety of animals—and even inedible objects—but they mainly eat the things they like: fish, sea turtles, seabirds, and marine mammals.

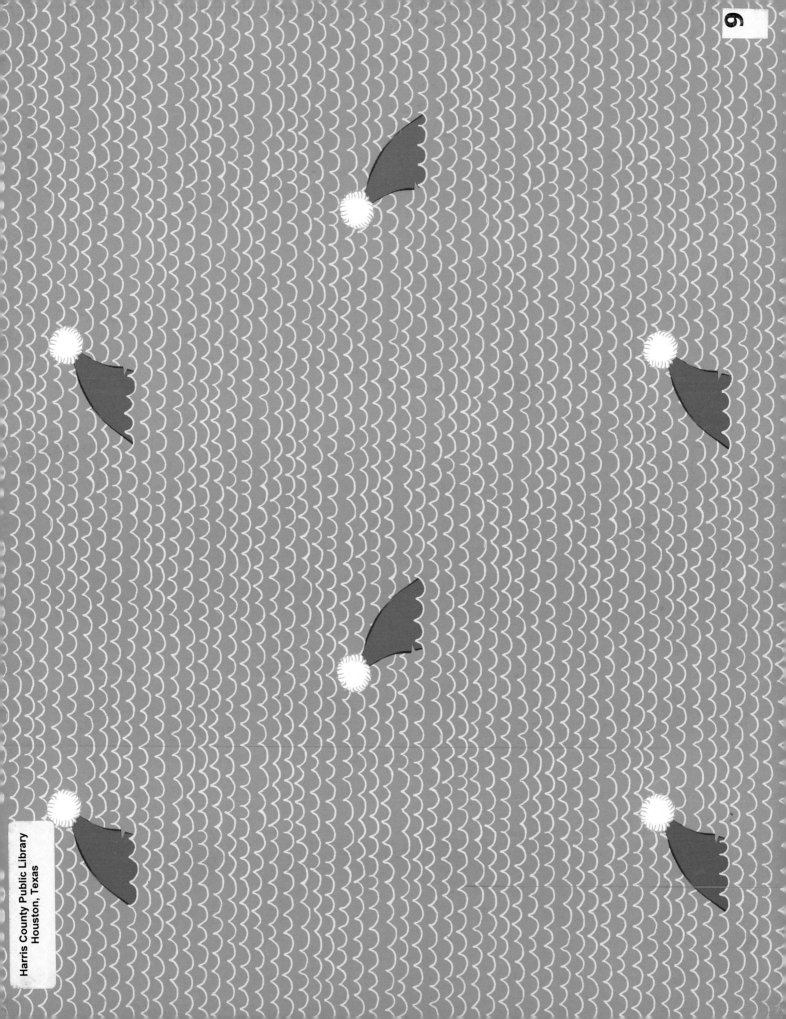